Berkshire

Edited By Allie Jones

First published in Great Britain in 2018 by:

Young Writers
Remus House
Coltsfoot Drive
Peterborough
PE2 9BF
Telephone: 01733 890066
Website: www.youngwriters.co.uk

All Rights Reserved
Book Design by Ashley Janson
© Copyright Contributors 2017
SB ISBN 978-1-78896-029-8
Printed and bound in the UK by BookPrintingUK
Website: www.bookprintinguk.com
YB0342T

FOREWORD

Welcome Reader, to Rhymecraft - Berkshire.

Among these pages you will find a whole host of poetic gems, built from the ground up by some wonderful young minds. Included are a variety of poetic styles, from amazing acrostics to creative cinquains, from dazzling diamantes to fascinating free verse.

Here at Young Writers our objective has always been to help children discover the joys of poetry and creative writing. Few things are more encouraging for the aspiring writer than seeing their own work in print. We are proud that our anthologies are able to give young authors this unique sense of confidence and pride in their abilities as well as letting their poetry reach new audiences.

The editing process was a tough but rewarding one that allowed us to gain an insight into the blooming creativity of today's primary school pupils. I hope you find as much enjoyment and inspiration in the following poetry as I have, so much so that you pick up a pen and get writing!

Allie Jones

CONTENTS

Battle Primary Academy, Reading

Morgan Edwards (7)	1
Nina Zovko (9)	2
Fode Victor Sadio (8)	3
Simileoluwa Amirat Ogunbadejo (9)	4
Hadia Bilal	6
Aisha Ayub (7)	7

Burghclere Primary School, Burghclere

Annabelle Wilson (8)	8
Ciara Langrell (8)	10
Jack Brooke Taylor (7)	11
Bertie Pilkington (8)	12
Dominic Webb (8)	13
Max Greenwell (7)	14
Lottie Morgan (9)	15
Grayson Arnold (8)	16
Pippa Owen (7)	17
Charlie Canning (8)	18
Lily Morgan (7)	19
Imogen Pickett (7)	20
Ezriann Solomon (8)	21
Dayzie Simpson (8)	22
Isabella Victoria Szafraniec-Coelho (8)	23
William Griffin (8)	24
Noah Lawley (7)	25
Rosie Higgs (8)	26

Evendons Primary School, Wokingham

Emma Oliver (7)	27
George Heath (7)	28

Hemdean House School, Caversham

Emma Sabin (9)	29
Eva Martha Peirce (9)	30
Advay Ajith Bhargava (9)	32
Helena Stevenson (9)	34
William Jenkins (8)	36
Arnav Sapkota (8)	38
Jennifer Voakes (11)	40
Theo Nichols (7)	41
Kian O'Brien (7)	42
Danny Massey (7)	43
Ashleigh Sabin (7) & Julia	44
Sulaiman T Al Sulaiman (7)	45

Horris Hill School, Newtown

Tamzin Brown (11)	46

Lambourn CE Primary School, Lambourn

Ashley Griffiths (9)	47
Oliver Morley (9)	48
Harmony White (10)	49
Charlie Howell (9)	50
Isabella Vermeulen Gouk (10)	51
Maisey Robinson (10)	52
Emily Willoughby (9)	53

Priory School, Slough

Name	Page
Yasmin Mansouri (10)	54
Aqsa Basit (9)	56
Millie Honey (10)	58
Carly Quigley (9)	60
Katie Jade Henderson (9)	62
Rishita Kondepudi (10)	64
Vinny Lane (10)	65
Charlie Owen (9)	66
Amaan Javed (10)	67
Ranveer Singh Wilkhu (9)	68
Cacee Nartey (8)	70
Eknoor Cheema (8)	71
Hannah Anaya (9)	72
Muhammad Faaiz-Ul-Haq (10)	73
Manveen Uppal (8)	74
Arwaa Kayani (9)	76
Abbygayle Ward (10)	77
Yousaf Sarwar (10)	78
Aron Arkosi (10)	79
Piper Owen (11)	80
Shazaib Mirza (10)	81
Katie Arthur-Robinson (10)	82
Muminah Ahmed (10)	83
Samuel Winyard (10)	84
Eisa Hussain (9)	85
Grace Downs (10)	86
Maria Tamimi (11)	87
Amisha Sharma (11)	88
Renu Fazal (9)	89
Hamzah Ahmed (10)	90
Sianna Amankwaah (10)	91
Sohan Miseer (10)	92
Olivia Prescott (8)	93
Khyla Powell Christian (8)	94
Fariha Hamza (9)	95
Tia Bradshaw (9)	96
Phoebe Olivia Ward (9)	97
Josh Akerman (10)	98
Mariam Hannah Khan (10)	99
Zara Khokhar (9)	100
Sam Arbouch (11)	101
Daniyal Akram (9)	102
Kylie Stanbridge (11)	103
Daanya McCarroll (8)	104
Aadam Qamar (9)	105
Aleena Syed (8)	106
Kirandeep Kaur Dhillon (9)	107
Charlette Barton-Johnson (10)	108
Katie Emery (10)	109
Cynthia R Machokoto (9)	110
Muhammad Moiz Khan (7)	111
Khushi Mishra (10)	112
Hira Basit (7)	113
Haris Shakir (9)	114
Marley-Rose Larkins (9)	115
Sharmaine Tianna Daryen Bevan (10)	116
Aminah Shakir (9)	117
Lexie Hiron (9)	118
Lia Santucci (11)	119
Shamaila Khan (9)	120
Jessica Roberts (9)	121
Amina Irfan (10)	122
Rehaan Ali (10)	123
Caitlin Nsubuga (11)	124
Naisha Mungur (10)	125
Amber-Lily Saunders (9)	126
Keelin Porter-Bull (10)	127
Eryka Grace Richardson (8)	128
Kiel Porter (10)	129
Alisha Rhea Khan (11)	130
Romany Donohoe-Flanders (7)	131
Saara Mahmood (9)	132
Rudaina Khan (9)	133
Alex-David Wande (9)	134
Ben Carter (7)	135
Mohamad Omar (8)	136
Cameron Haines (10)	137
Shayaan Ahmed (9)	138

St Paul's Catholic Primary School, Tilehurst

Lottie Stretton (8)	139
Molly Clift (7)	140
Sophia Armstrong (8)	141
Harry Meaden (9)	142
Ava Slade (9)	143
Charley Pearson (8)	144
Alissa Shoefield (8)	145
Stephanie Adaugo Ugochukwu (7)	146
Erin Crawford (7)	147
Kayla Patton (8)	148
Callum Barrow (8)	149

THE POEMS

Football, Football, Football

Football, football, football.
Messi, Neymar and Ronaldo.
Travel around the world and play for their clubs
They will go.
The best sport in the world.
Teams play here and there.
Some will shout and cheer
And others will cry in tears.
Football trophies everywhere,
At the end winners will be declared.

Football, what a good game,
Kick and scream, start with a warm up,
Training can be the key to a successful team.
We walk on the pitch and fall in a ditch.
Oh no, one player is hurt.
He got hurt on his foot.
The game with only 10 players.
The game finished with a smile,
Who knows what will happen in a while?

Morgan Edwards (7)
Battle Primary Academy, Reading

Dreams

Dreams are bad and dreams are good,
They put me in a totally great mood,
Some are scary, some are sunny,
Some are even quite funny.

Some are fun and some have drama,
Some are going wacky bananas,
Their endings are good and bad,
Some are making me quite mad.

Some might have scary mythical creatures,
But might have quite good features,
They have a good or bad story,
But might not be the best as the movie with Dory.

You might dream of getting a dog with a collar,
But maybe you win a million dollars,
That's all for now and I say goodbye.

Nina Zovko (9)
Battle Primary Academy, Reading

Science

Astronomy,
Involves some chemistry,
You go and study at university,
When studying you say to yourself
Of course it's true
You say to yourself, *I don't believe you!*

So you go and study physics
You thought that hydrogen does gymnastics
Dumb, yow!
It ain't true
So you gave up on that.

Two things aren't for you,
So what should you do?
Try again of course!
Because...
Resilience is key!

Fode Victor Sadio (8)
Battle Primary Academy, Reading

Always United

The Earth together
Standing as one
The Earth together
Have some fun.

There are good times and bad times
We may fight
But standing together
We stick tight.

We're all united
That is the key
We're all united
You and me.

There won't always be peace
But look in your heart
Not a single cheat
Can keep it apart.

We're all united
That is the key

We're united
You and me.

Simileoluwa Amirat Ogunbadejo (9)
Battle Primary Academy, Reading

Potion Full Of Love For Friends!

You don't have a friend?
Cos of a fight which made you bend.

I'll get someone for you to love,
Make you fly like a dove!

You'll both have big hearts
And memorable parts.

Your faces will be as white as snow
And in your hair will be a big red bow.

You'll be together forever,
BFFs forever!

Hadia Bilal
Battle Primary Academy, Reading

Bad Dreams And Good Dreams!

I had a dream
That was very mean.

About a clown
That was pulling us down.

He was greedy
Also needy.

A unicorn came
And saved the day.

Everyone had a smile on their face
And were crowded in a pile.

They went home
With a phone.

Aisha Ayub (7)
Battle Primary Academy, Reading

Pets

It's hard getting up in the morning,
I have to do the chickens,
Why does it have to be me? I say,
Why can't it just be my sis?

I have to take care of the cat don't forget,
Feed him, wash him, clean him out,
Sometimes I wish I could have no pets,
But they are kind of cute.

The chickens and cat are a lot of work,
I wonder why Mummy chose me,
Why not Sissy? She's just like me and you,
Life is really hard with pets.

Waking me up to do the little chicks,
It's just ridiculously hard,
I'd rather be in bed,
This is nothing like the kiddie life, I thought.

I thought it would be luscious,
Drinking tea and biscuits,

I guess not,
Seriously, *why me?*

Annabelle Wilson (8)
Burghclere Primary School, Burghclere

Me And My Best Friend...

Me and my best friend...
Love to dance and prance all day.
What is your hobby?

Me and my best friend...
Sing like Rihanna all day.
What is your hobby?

Me and my best friend...
Use our imagination.
What is your hobby?

Me and my best friend...
Make dens with blankets.
What is your hobby?

Do you and your best friend have a hobby?

Ciara Langrell (8)
Burghclere Primary School, Burghclere

Riddle Of Animals

This animal is the king of the forest,
It hunts in prides,
It is a meat eater.
It is... the lion.

This animal is the fastest land animal,
It has spots,
Its claws never retract.
Yes it is... the cheetah.

This animal lives in the sea,
It lives in Antarctica,
It has a beak.
Yes it is... the penguin.

Jack Brooke Taylor (7)
Burghclere Primary School, Burghclere

Sea Creatures

You can get...
Red fish,
Green fish,
Orange fish,
Blue fish.
Where?

You can get...
Yellow sharks,
Pink sharks,
Purple sharks,
Turquoise sharks.
Where?

You can get...
Black squid,
Grey squid,
White squid,
Brown squid.
Where?

Under the sea of course!

Bertie Pilkington (8)
Burghclere Primary School, Burghclere

School

School is cool
Because there are summer fetes,
I can also see all my mates.

We were learning to spell the number two,
I asked to go to the loo
So that I could have a poo.

If you don't go to school
That means you are a fool
Because you get to play ball.

School is cool!

Dominic Webb (8)
Burghclere Primary School, Burghclere

Spider-Man

I have seen Spider-Man,
he was climbing a building.
I have seen Spider-Man,
he was swinging from a building.
I have seen Spider-Man,
and he was beating up a bad boy.
I have seen Spider-Man,
and he was jumping between buildings.
I have seen Spider-Man,
and he was beating up bad men.

Max Greenwell (7)
Burghclere Primary School, Burghclere

The Loo

The loo is my worst enemy,
I wish it wasn't invented,
I say to myself,
'The pot was much better,
'Cause it didn't have a flush,
They just tipped it out the window,
Nobody really cared.'
People say I'm a bit old-fashioned,
But I don't really mind.

Lottie Morgan (9)
Burghclere Primary School, Burghclere

Minecraft

Come on, come on, Minecraft awaits!
With a whole universe to explore.
With blocky monsters in the night.
Don't rush, don't rush, it's a really good game.
With mods like the Pokémon mod
And bring your friends, adventure awaits!

Grayson Arnold (8)
Burghclere Primary School, Burghclere

The Rainbow Brick

Red in bed.
Orange in the sun.
Blue is cold.
Yellow is cool in the sun.
Green is graceful.
Pink is friends with purple
But purple goes in a circle.
White is wet.
Black is sick.
Turquoise has a tan.
Maroon is mundane.

Pippa Owen (7)
Burghclere Primary School, Burghclere

Football

Football is a sport.
Football is about teamwork.
Football is about passing.
Football is about respect.
Football is about scoring.
Football is about saving goals.
Football is about taking part.
Football is about being a team player.

Charlie Canning (8)
Burghclere Primary School, Burghclere

What Is It?

It has a pointy bit on it.
Sometimes it can fly.
It loves to help people
When it comes to friendship problems.
It is very kind and friendly.
Sometimes princesses ride it.
What is it?

Answer: A unicorn.

Lily Morgan (7)
Burghclere Primary School, Burghclere

Raindrops

Rain makes me feel cross,
It makes me wet and cold,
It dribbles down my arms
And it splashes around my toes.
It makes me very soggy,
I wish I was dry,
I would like the rain to stop
Falling from the sky.

Imogen Pickett (7)
Burghclere Primary School, Burghclere

What Am I?

It has a shell.
It can go underwater.
It is playful.
It can glide underwater.
Sometimes it stays on land.
You can find it by the ocean.
What is it?

Answer: A turtle.

Ezriann Solomon (8)
Burghclere Primary School, Burghclere

The Netball Star!

Nelly is a netballer,
Shooting lots of goals,
Whenever she's gone,
We all go bong!
The boys go ding!
The girls go dong!
The referee goes mad
Because the game's so bad.

Dayzie Simpson (8)
Burghclere Primary School, Burghclere

Animals And Seal

A nnie,
N atty,
I zzy,
M e,
A ll
L ove
S eals.

S eals
E at
A qua
L impets.

Isabella Victoria Szafraniec-Coelho (8)
Burghclere Primary School, Burghclere

Devils Do

Devils do what devils do,
In the Underworld,
Daring us and daring you,
For the fun of dare
Devils do what devils do.

William Griffin (8)
Burghclere Primary School, Burghclere

Fuzzy Bear

Cuddle wobbly bears.
Fussy wussy bears.
Pinky winky bears.
Fluffy wuffy bears.
Sweet, sweet bears.

Noah Lawley (7)
Burghclere Primary School, Burghclere

Pineapples

Pineapple, pineapple
Tangy tang,
Imagine cats,
Eating pineapples!

Rosie Higgs (8)
Burghclere Primary School, Burghclere

Friendship

F riends forever
R unning together
I won't let our friendship split
E ven if we get split apart, my best friend will be in my heart
N ever will our friendship end
D oing all the things we love
S inging is one of the things we do together
H elping each other at school
I love her ever so much
P leasing her makes me smile for when we are together we're always happy because we're best friends forever!

Emma Oliver (7)
Evendons Primary School, Wokingham

Things In The Jungle - Haiku

Monkeys in the trees
Parrots squeaking, butterflies
Hyenas hunting.

George Heath (7)
Evendons Primary School, Wokingham

My Hot And Cold Poem!

Hot is burning, no one can stand it.
Everyone hates it and does not like it a bit.
Hot is not cold, cold is not hot.
No one can stand the cold, not even a bot.
Cold is freezing, cold is icicles and snow,
When it's cold Santa goes, 'Ho ho!'
Is it hot or is it cold?
None of these are bold!
When it's cold, bring a fluffy coat,
Do not bring a toy boat.
There are freezing temperatures in the water,
The Death Valley is much hotter.
When you're in the sun too long
You'll get a sunburn,
When you get a sunburn it's a great concern.
Some places that have icicles that look like crystal,
When you shoot a pistol at a crystal,
It will turn into a puddle.
When it's hot the sun shines bright,
You will never reach the sun's height!

Emma Sabin (9)
Hemdean House School, Caversham

My Special Box
(Based on 'The Magic Box' by Kit Wright)

I will put in my box...
The most warm and beautiful cloak of crushed Venice velvet.
An elegant, golden dragon swishing by.
An incredible day with the sun glancing down
and an upset little girl having a sigh.

I will put in my box...
A lovely, white singing lark chirping in the morning.
A little girl with hair as gold as the sun.
A small but perfect sweet shop
and the finest freshly baked bun.

I will put in my box...
The start of every super sunny day.
A tree filled with apples to feed the poor.
The crisp, beautiful calmness of an open space
and a teacher who opens your learning door.

I will put in my box...
My first birthday presents because they
were magical.

A bird in a ballet studio.
A flying ballet dancer
and a fat, smiling pet crocodile.

My box is fashioned from
A book as big as the world.
The purest of pearls from the Atlantic.
The most polished diamonds are in the corners
and it is scrubbed by a small lick.

I shall sing in my box,
in front of the crowds in the Sydney Opera House,
but really I like to sing with nature,
so that is why I will sing with a baby fox.

Eva Martha Peirce (9)
Hemdean House School, Caversham

The Magic Box
(Based on 'The Magic Box' by Kit Wright)

I will put in the box...
A pinch of magical cuddly cotton to make my sleep
peaceful and magical.
A whoosh of a legendary dark monster
helping a hero.
Creepy crowded crocodiles munching the grass.

I will put in the box...
A blue sun on a stormy night.
A shapeless insect as huge as me
and a glass of sparkling orange water
from the top of the giant building Burj Khalifa.

I will put in the box...
Five interesting sentences spoken in an unknown
language.
A dazzling spark from a ferocious fish
and a unique giant as small as a bird
stomping and banging through a forbidden
and unknown place.

I will put into the box...
The first cute statement of a glorious baby.
The final laugh of a grandpa
and the last beautiful story of an uncle.

My box is fashioned from
Tremendous gold, silver and aluminium,
with ancient light from above.
Its corners are amazing crystal stars
and its edges are diamond chocolates.

I shall fly in my box
From the great Empire State Building
to my home then all the way to anywhere.

Advay Ajith Bhargava (9)
Hemdean House School, Caversham

My Magic Box
(Based on 'The Magic Box' by Kit Wright)

I will put in the box...
An adventurous ape that's eaten a shiny apple,
with the affect of an alarming alien.
The appearance of an amazing author.

I will put in the box...
A bad banished big boom
or a good, big Blue Peter badge
peacefully resting with a huge bang from a bed.

I will put in the box...
A crazy, mad cat, as cool as a cucumber,
with a small cake for a camel,
a card from a criminal crocodile that got sent
at Christmas.

I will put in the box...
A dangling, dangerous diary
as tall as a daffodil that wouldn't dilly dally.
A DIY man who was always so tired,
with a lonely old dog that fixes things.

My box is fashioned from
Long stringy elastic bands,
with power from electricity bouncing through it.
My box will have 100 eyelashes crafted as hinges.

I shall fix my box with
Thrilling fancy foxes.
I will feel much more fresh
then I will stay there for a fortnight feeling so fine.

Helena Stevenson (9)
Hemdean House School, Caversham

The Magic Box
(Based on 'The Magic Box' by Kit Wright)

I will put in the box...
Some cuddly cotton that was inside a pillow.
A magical meerkat from a hot desert.
A silky seal from the Atlantic Ocean.

I will put in the box...
A slice of brown chocolate cake talking to me.
A mint choc chip cake shouting loudly to me.
A slice of cheesecake spitting cheese at me.

I will put in the box...
Dele Alli driving a fast Formula 1 car.
William Shakespeare singing a song.
Lewis Hamilton playing football.

I will put in the box...
A teddy that is soft silk.
A toy shark that is really fast at swimming.
A toy owl that is really good at flying.

My box is fashioned from
Rose gold and shining diamonds.
Crystal-clear iron and shiny bronze.
Beautiful patterns all around the box.

I shall
Fly high in the sky like a pretty bird.
Colours like orange and yellow in the sky.
Fantastic shiny stars like sparkling diamonds in the sky.

William Jenkins (8)
Hemdean House School, Caversham

I Will Put In The Box

(Based on 'The Magic Box' by Kit Wright)

I will put in the box...
Lovely lavishing liquorice leaving Lindors.
Silver silk sari slinging slingshots.
Dreadful Dracula dining on Daniel.

I will put in the box...
Evil Aunty Cabbage gobbling up boiled cabbages.
The blackness of a black hole.
A slice of brown chocolate cake talking to me like a dog.

I will put in the box...
Three amazing wishes in Chinese.
A dozen genies rising from the dead.
A gorgeous glistening grandad.

I will put in the box...
Oliver Noorwood in a rapid F1 car
and Lewis Hamilton playing football
and the car reading a newspaper.

My box is fashioned from
Titanium to steel and Arctic ice to gold,
and the corners are ball-shaped.
Made of titanium and buckets of ice.

I shall
Surf in my box.
Ride a pony and dance my heart out to the world
and *bang!* Chewing gum has appeared.

Arnav Sapkota (8)
Hemdean House School, Caversham

Autumn

Y ippee! A shower of leaves!
E xciting festivals are on their way
L arge branches start to fall
L ots of birthdays come in autumn
O ff goes the sparkly fireworks
W ebs glisten in the sunlight

G reen leaves stay on the tree
R abbits come, foxes hunt
E ating pumpkin pie, time to share
E njoy parties with your friends
N ever forget your raincoat

R ainy weather starts to come
E very coat will do
D on't forget the gloves.

Jennifer Voakes (11)
Hemdean House School, Caversham

Six Ways Of Looking At The Moon

The moon is an old man and his face is lit up against the dark night sky.
The moon is an alien spaceship spinning in space.
The moon is a banana that aliens eat for dinner.
The moon is a silver frying pan tossed into the air by the gods.
The moon is a letter C thrown into the air by the anger of the gods.
The moon is a leftover pie from the alien's dinner.
I've always wanted to visit the moon.

Theo Nichols (7)
Hemdean House School, Caversham

Six Ways Of Looking At The Moon

The moon is a spherical whiteboard moving across the dark floor.
The moon is a marble moving across the tarmac.
The moon is a big white ball of cheese rolling across a carpet.
The moon is a banana with aliens on it.
The moon is a starry sphere thingy with lava tunnels.
The moon is a big ball of white snow making endless silence.
I love the moon!

Kian O'Brien (7)
Hemdean House School, Caversham

Five Ways Of Looking At The Moon

The moon is a marble moving on a dark floor.
The moon is a big white ball of cheese rolling across a dark carpet.
The moon is a banana with aliens on.
The moon is a starry, spherical planet with lava.
The moon is a big ball of white snow making endless silence.
I like the moon and I want to visit the moon.

Danny Massey (7)
Hemdean House School, Caversham

Six Ways Of Looking At The Moon

The moon is a grey ball in a black box.
The moon is a marble rolling across a black
and dark floor.
The moon is a grey thumbprint.
The moon is a big sphere shining in the sky.
The moon is a ghostly galleon on the dark sea.
The moon is a grey, rocky sphere.
I love the moon so much!

Ashleigh Sabin (7) & Julia
Hemdean House School, Caversham

Three Ways Of Looking At The Moon

The moon is a big sphere spinning in the sky.
The moon is grey and black with astronauts visiting it.
The moon is a place to jump on.

Sulaiman T Al Sulaiman (7)
Hemdean House School, Caversham

The Great Wonder Of Horses

Animals come in all shapes and sizes,
all colours and creations,
especially the powerful, beautiful horse,
they're my favourite.
Their beauty is no match for other creatures.
They are majestic, also very intelligent
and an extremely speedy runner too.

They come in a variety of colours
which are black, white and brown.
If you like them, choose one!
Around the track it goes,
as fast as no one knows.
Wandering through the forest,
with great big trees.
Near the waterfall where it prances and leaps
with its friend
and that's the very end!

Tamzin Brown (11)
Horris Hill School, Newtown

Minecraft, The Game Of Imagination!

M inecraft is a game of imagination and creativity.
 I ncredible pixelated graphics.
N ight-time play is risky, watch out for the zombies!
E nchanted range of weapons, tools and armour.
C reepers are to be avoided.
R apid gameplay adventures from biome to biome.
A wesome villages to explore and worlds full of colour.
F un, friendly online challenges.
T he game where you are in charge of your own destiny.

Ashley Griffiths (9)
Lambourn CE Primary School, Lambourn

Creepers Are Out!

Creepers are out
Creepers about
Creepers are out with no doubt
Very green
Very keen
Very seldom seen

They're behind you
And they will find you
What would you do
Run from them
Hide from them
Avoid them
Put glass in front of them
They can't see through glass
They should make glasses out of the glass
But if you hear *boom, boom, boom!*
It's your doom, doom, doom!

Oliver Morley (9)
Lambourn CE Primary School, Lambourn

Swish, Swish

Swish, swish! There was a fish.
Down by the lake I saw a snake.
In the bog I saw a frog.
Down the road I saw a blue-lipped toad.

Buzz, buzz! There was a honeybee.
Up in the tree I saw a chimpanzee.
In the night sky I saw an owl fly by.
In the middle of a gale I saw a giant snail.

Moo, moo! The cow said, 'Boo!'

Harmony White (10)
Lambourn CE Primary School, Lambourn

Dragon Egg

Chickens and pigs can help us live,
creepers and zombies destroy our buildings,
it's time to get revenge.
Pack your bags with enough
to help you defend yourself and live.
While the rest of the party keep digging.

Find the end portal, jump in,
defeat the fierce dragon
and to return home
with a dragon egg to tame the beast.

Charlie Howell (9)
Lambourn CE Primary School, Lambourn

Time

Tick-tock! goes that clock.
Time is precious, time is true.
Time is the one thing we should all be devoted to.
You can't slow it down.
You can't speed it up.
Time you should never waste,
As time always makes haste.
Let's just make the most of the time we have got.
Tick-tock! goes that clock.

Isabella Vermeulen Gouk (10)
Lambourn CE Primary School, Lambourn

Mr White Had A Fright

Mr White had a fright,
In the middle of the night.
He saw a ghost eating toast,
Halfway up a lamp post.
The ghost came down
And went to town
In his dressing gown.
The ghost was a host for a quiz show,
Everyone's score was low
So he said, 'Go!'
To a girl wearing a bow.

Maisey Robinson (10)
Lambourn CE Primary School, Lambourn

Many Clouds

Even though he's laid to rest
He ran his heart out and did his best.

Now he's gone but not forgotten
The sport of racing sometimes can be rotten.

Emily Willoughby (9)
Lambourn CE Primary School, Lambourn

Emotions

Anger
The anger inside me makes me feel so bad
I just don't understand why I feel so mad
When I hear the word 'anger'
I think of the colour red
It's like a whole big fire starting in my head.

Sadness
The sadness inside me makes me feel so blue
I guess I'm just glad this hasn't happened to you
No one can outrun sadness
Unless of course you're filled with happiness.

Happiness
The happiness inside me is too good to be real
Do you understand how amazing I feel?
Most people prefer happiness over the rest
And personally I think that it's the best.

Fear
The fear inside me is nothing but fright
The feeling of butterflies is really not right
Fear is like a scary story

While your cheeks flash red
It's like that story of a monster under your bed!

Emotions are a wonderful thing
But I promise you light will always win!

Yasmin Mansouri (10)
Priory School, Slough

Stupendous, Sensational Seasons

In summer, it gets hot and burning,
It feels wonderful when we go swimming.
We can play or we can rest,
We can do anything before sunset.
We go on vacation on lovely beaches
And have fun eating some yummy peaches.

Then comes autumn,
You may call it 'fall'.
The leaves from trees, they start to fall.
It gets chilly as the days progress,
But not as chilly as it gets.

Then comes the mighty winter,
So cold and freezing,
If you go outside without a coat
You'll start sneezing.
Strong and cold winds blow,
Will they blow us along?
We don't know.

And then it's time for spring,
Oh sweet, sunny, breezy spring.
It's time for the flowers to bloom
And plants to grow.
You can hear birds chirp
And people sing.
That is what we call spring.

Aqsa Basit (9)
Priory School, Slough

Music That Haunts Them

A boy had a dream
But soon enough it came true.
Couldn't wait for X Factor,
Don't we all have dreams, do you?

Eager to find a friend she started busking,
Friends can be enemies you know,
'Get ready,' she says, 'I'm coming.'
He is too.

In the night he was searching for her,
Jennifer her name was,
Kind is one word but she is another,
Luke is my name and music haunts me.

My name is Jennifer
And my life was normal,
Not a worry in my life but...
Oh my music haunts me.

Punching isn't nice but it happens anyways,
Queens and kings rule but not over them,

Rubies and diamonds are no good too,
Stop them before music haunts everyone.

Millie Honey (10)
Priory School, Slough

My Auntie's Rabbits

One bunny is called Harvey
And the other Likey Lou,
That's right, you've guessed it,
My auntie has two.

They live in my auntie's kitchen
And lounge about all day,
Their bed is warm and cosy
As it is made of hay.

They are my auntie's babies,
She loves them very much,
But when they are naughty
She kicks them into touch.

Their skin is soft and furry just like silk,
They always drink water and never touch milk.

They are very timid animals,
They don't like a lot of noise,
Except when they are playing with their toys.

If I had another life a bunny I would be,
Because their life is more laid back,
I'd see things differently.

Carly Quigley (9)
Priory School, Slough

Seasons

Spring
The blossom fills the trees,
While the wind blows a warm breeze,
Lambs are calling,
Creatures are crawling.

Summer
School is over, the sun is out,
Me and my family are out and about,
Enjoy the warmth while it's here,
Autumn is about to appear.

Autumn
The leaves are changing to a reddish brown,
The light is starting to dim down,
The air is now feeling cool
But yet again I'm back at school.

Winter
The frost is clinging,
The bells are ringing,
I can see Santa's sleigh
And hear the singing.

The year is coming to an end,
Don't worry spring's on its way again.

Katie Jade Henderson (9)
Priory School, Slough

Candy Land

C andy Land, Candy Land, everything's sweets, everything's sweets
A ll is sweet, no need to weep, don't worry, this is all cheap.
N eed your veggies, there are vegetable sweets, also with a dip of honey.
D on't worry, we've got fruits too, the sweetest you can find, you can't resist.
Y ou'll always have the best time and chew a toothpaste sweet every time.

L ove it, show to your friends and share this fun with everyone.
A void the marshmallows, you cannot resist and don't forget the chocolate volcanoes.
N o more worries, you'll have the best for no one can beat your candy quest.
D o limit yourself, too much isn't good!

Rishita Kondepudi (10)
Priory School, Slough

Lego In The Shops

Bricks of red and bricks of blue,
Stick together as if using glue,
Little pieces in yellow or green,
Lots and lots at the shops,
But the kids will not be clean,
The worker comes to open the door,
'A flood! A flood!' he screams quite loud.
'No, it's us, you fool!'
Replies a child from the crowd.
'Look here, look here!' a little girl cries,
'The Lego is here! It's by the pies!'

That night, the kids are gone, along with the Lego,
The aisles are silent.
As for the worker,
He is at home with his own Lego.
As he builds, he remembers,
The smiling faces of the children,
This was true happiness.

Vinny Lane (10)
Priory School, Slough

The Best Mummy

My mummy makes me proud,
with all the things she does.
My mummy makes me happy, whenever I am sad.
My mummy is the best, in every single way.
My mummy makes sure she has the time for me.
My mummy loves chocolate...
it's her favourite treat.
My mummy likes Diet Coke,
because she loves the fizz.
My mummy loves Chinese food,
her favourite is sweet chilli beef.
My mummy loves eating,
it's her favourite thing to do.
My mummy and I love playing Super Mario Bros
and playing basketball in the garden.
We love playing board games
and a little bit of Lego.
Our favourite thing to do
is to spend time with each other.

Charlie Owen (9)
Priory School, Slough

Freedom

You can wear what you want,
Fight for what you see,
We're all equal and that's how it should be.
We will not be segregated, holding hands together,
People are all the same,
We shall be forever.
We can lead like a king or rule like Gandhi!
If you are from Kenya or Palestine,
France or Germany,
We are all the same, on life's journey.
Life is all about love,
We were made to be together,
Like pancakes and syrup,
Pen and paper.
Peace is there so now let's use it,
Segregation; we should try to lose it.
So take a look and see beyond this,
Into a life of freedom and justice.

Amaan Javed (10)
Priory School, Slough

The Sounds Of Nature

Mother Nature left a bag,
Coloured blue and green,
She left a note saying:
'Open it and see'.

The blanket of the fog,
The rumble of the volcano,
The tapping of the rain,
The shining of the sun.

The swirling of the tornado,
The trembling of the Earth,
The swaying of the grass,
The howling of the wind.

The fluttering of the snowflakes,
The drumming of the thunder,
The rustling of the leaves,
The waves of the ocean.

Mother Nature left a bag,
Coloured blue and green:

'Take care of the world,
Love it, cherish it and nourish it for me'.

Ranveer Singh Wilkhu (9)
Priory School, Slough

Stars Shining Bright Tonight

Stars shining bright tonight,
Always make the dark sky brighter,
Your leader who guides you
Is the lovely white moon,
Who shines the brightest of them all,
If you join us we make beautiful pictures,
We can help you find your way around,
Stars shine all over the dark sky,
If it wasn't for you and the moon
We wouldn't be able to see in the dark.
You shine so bright,
Just like the bright sky.
Stars, you're so amazing, we love you so much,
I could just hug you all in my beautiful arms,
Stars, you're so bright, marvellous and sparkly,
You help us so much and we love you all.

Cacee Nartey (8)
Priory School, Slough

Sing, Sing, Sing

Sing, sing, sing to set you free.
Sing, sing, sing so you can see.
Sing, sing, sing to light up the world.
Sing, sing, sing to hear every word.
Sing, sing, sing so Mother Nature can hear.
Sing, sing, sing to everyone that's near.
Sing, sing, sing so everybody knows.
Sing, sing, sing where everybody goes.
Sing, sing, sing to give a cheer.
Sing, sing, sing to all the hares.
Sing, sing, sing because you don't care.
Sing, sing, sing during your dare.
Sing, sing, sing to all the deer.
Sing, sing, sing to all that's there.
Sing, sing, sing because singing is what we do!

Eknoor Cheema (8)
Priory School, Slough

Polar Bears

P is for precious (and sort of harmless) creatures
O is for optimism because I believe we can put a stop to their endangerment
L is for love that I give to these poor creatures
A is for amazing animals that should be appreciated and cared for
R is for royal, majestic bears who rule the Arctic

B is for brilliant animals who shall one day live in tranquillity
E is for endangered creatures that fight to live every day
A is for astonishing things these bears do
R is for recovery that can only be achieved if we take action *now!*

Hannah Anaya (9)
Priory School, Slough

The Dark And Light Reunion

Dark and light have been together for years
Like strawberry and vanilla or bread and honey.

Dark is like another nightmare,
Taking over, so cold and bare
But give it a chance, you may be afraid,
Give it some time, it will be light again.

Dark over light.
Light over dark.
But don't be scared, dark doesn't bite,
Not a single shark in sight.

But if it was light forever
How would we sleep?
And wouldn't it be boring
And we would all weep.
So who do you think will win?
They are waiting to come out of the dragon's den!

Muhammad Faaiz-Ul-Haq (10)
Priory School, Slough

My Dreams

It's time for bed again.
As my head rests on the pillow
And my eyes close
I go into a world
That nobody knows.

I see unicorns
And butterflies too,
Munching on flowers
With sparkly blue shoes.

As I step forward
I see my friends waving at me,
I step closer
They turn into fairies
And fly into a tree.

When I see pandas
I fall in love,
Penguins, cheetahs, leopards
And beautiful white doves.

I open my eyes
There's nothing to be seen
Then I realise
It was all just a dream.

Manveen Uppal (8)
Priory School, Slough

The Amazon Rainforest

The Amazon rainforest, the breathtaking view,
the countable species, the exploring that's new.

The exotic and fragranced flowers,
the glistening sea.

The chameleon tongue-like leaves,
the tall towering trees.

The majestic birds, the colourful feathers,
the sunset-coloured beak, the humid weather.

The graceful swans, the fragile flow,
the ivory-white feathers, the water that's shallow.

The multicoloured butterfly, the symmetrical wings,
the delicate flying, as valuable as a golden ring.

Arwaa Kayani (9)
Priory School, Slough

Emotions

All of my emotions,
Are spilling out of my head onto this page,
They mix into potions,
Lime green, neon yellow and red rage.

A smile begins to spread across my face,
My eyes are shining bright,
I prance across the room with grace,
This is joy! I think to myself
As I walk up to the window and look out
To the still Saturday night.

A single tear runs down my face,
My hands are shaking, this doesn't feel right,
I feel scared as I walk through this place,
I swivel around to see a big fright.

Abbygayle Ward (10)
Priory School, Slough

Life

Life is something we all live in
Whether we are fat or thin
But we still live happily with our kin.

We need wool, grab the shears!
Some fellow helped us and we said, 'Cheers!'
We can now sleep in our beds with no fears.

You can grow up bad,
Be a helpful dad
Or just be an intellectual lad!

Be as tall as a plane
Or as small as a candy cane
But just remember we are all the same.

For our family, we must cook,
While you wait, maybe read a book
But remember to keep a look.

Yousaf Sarwar (10)
Priory School, Slough

The Nether And The End

There was life, there was death,
All this excitement and noise almost made me deaf.

Once I said, 'I'm the best, forget the rest.'
I went down a cave, got some lava
And quickly jumped on my llama.

I went down to the Nether,
Got some soul sand,
Killed some withers with my dime,
Told my people no man left behind.

Went to the end, no enchanted armour,
Told the dragon, 'Bug off you darner!'

This is the end of my story,
Now stop playing and watch Finding Dory.

Aron Arkosi (10)
Priory School, Slough

The Life Of A Dreamer

A dream is a wonderful word.
It doesn't come in a herd!
I would like to dream of unicorns and ice cream
For in the day I will forget what it means.

Dreaming is something you do in the night
Because without dreams there is no light.
In the day we dream of chocolate galore
For the night I will forget what I adore.

Dreams are something you shouldn't ignore
Because they can help you unlock a door.
With the thing you like more.
For you should know
You should always dream like no one else can.

Piper Owen (11)
Priory School, Slough

A Game Of Death

I turn around and take a look,
At how many lives they took,
You are so stupid, read a book,
Once we threaten you, you'll be shook.
As they charge, we charge too,
Even though we don't know,
What they will do.
Then a centaur shoots an arrow,
And even comes a big black sparrow.
We all commence the dangerous battle,
As we hear the ogres cackle.
I don't want to fight,
Even though I'm a knight.
I'm the last one,
Along with another
But I killed him
And his name was Tim.

Shazaib Mirza (10)
Priory School, Slough

First Snow

In anticipation, he taps his claws,
With his tail wagging - I open the doors,
He stops, frozen in fright,
Before him, a blanket of white.

With his lead, being pulled,
An ivory sea, tempting him - being called.
He has no choice but to dive,
And it turns out... he starts to thrive!

Frosty flakes start to fall,
The piles of winter start to grow tall,
His paws finding a way through,
So many wonderful things to do.

In this white land,
The trees sway in a wintry band.

Katie Arthur-Robinson (10)
Priory School, Slough

Emotions

Emotions can come and go
Whether you are alone
Or when you are in a crowd
Emotions, emotions here I come
Will you pick me
Or will you pick someone else in the world?

When I am sad the sadness
Can only be unlocked by my heart
And I am the only one
Who can cheer myself up.

When I am happy I know my position
And I can keep in contact with my friends.

When I am angry I can smash things
And snap things up
But I am trying to keep myself cheered up.

Muminah Ahmed (10)
Priory School, Slough

My House Of Hope

All alone in the woods,
Build a shelter said my mind,
Climbing up to my new future,
Destroying trees to get some wood,
Endless snow covers me like an ice-cold blanket,
Foraging for food and drink,
Growing weaker as the day goes by,
How could I possibly survive this season of doom?
Ice grows freezing water in the blink of an eye,
Justice has lost me completely now,
Knowing how to finally build my home of hope,
Lingering around my new wooden walls,
Might I just survive this winter now?

Samuel Winyard (10)
Priory School, Slough

My Bike

My bike is called Spike.
My bike is really cool,
He does wheelies in a pool.
Sometimes he's a fool,
But when we ride he is very cool.

When we go down a hill,
We never stop until we are still.
I will ride it on the road,
And when I press hard on the brake,
I would go flying off the seat.

I'll learn new tricks,
And learn them well.
When I fall I can still stand up,
And feel tall.

My bike is so cool,
I ride it to school.

Eisa Hussain (9)
Priory School, Slough

Dreams

Everyone has a dream,
Singing or dancing or anything really.
It's even more amazing though
When it comes true,
Standing right in front of you,
Your dream, just imagine that,
And when you see that,
That is that,
Now you can say,
My dream, my dream has come true,
The best, wow, it's the best,
And God whispers in your ear, 'It's your future.'
Take the chance, you only have one,
Go up the stairs not down,
So always remember,
Your dream will come true.

Grace Downs (10)
Priory School, Slough

Haunted

The boy stands alone.
His head pounding, trying to forget
about the things he has been through.
People tormenting him and mocking him,
yet he still has hope.

A girl stands alone.
She says that her worst nightmares
are coming true.
Others say she's a psycho,
yet she still has hope.

Some people think it's alright
to make people afraid wherever they go
but many take it too far.

We all stand alone.
We are all equal.

Maria Tamimi (11)
Priory School, Slough

Galactic Space!

All night and day I dream of space,
I see the stars dancing in grace,
We all look up to the dark blue sky
Then we all say goodbye.

The moon shines bright,
It's blinding light,
What a sight,
For one dark night.

Mars is red,
Like food dyed bread,
For you and me, it could be
The darkest planet that may be.

Galactic space, galactic space,
For I only see you all night,
You shine your light
And then I say goodnight.

Amisha Sharma (11)
Priory School, Slough

Blackbeard, Blackbeard

Blackbeard, Blackbeard sails on the
Queen Anne's Revenge.
Blackbeard, Blackbeard travels the sea
to scavenge.
Blackbeard, Blackbeard looks for war.
Blackbeard, Blackbeard, blood, guts and gore.
Blackbeard, Blackbeard kills his mate for treasure.
Blackbeard, Blackbeard, for greed and pleasure.
Blackbeard, Blackbeard is now under pressure.
Blackbeard, Blackbeard is all alone.
Blackbeard, Blackbeard is now slaughtered.

Renu Fazal (9)
Priory School, Slough

Rapping Life

Life isn't all about bling, bling,
Even though I've got a 24 carat gold ring, ring,
I've got a Lambo
But that's not what life's all about bro.

People call me Fat Man,
Bruh!
That's what they are in the mirror.
They try to diss me,
But they're just a fatso.

I have a friend
But we broke up,
I wish we could make amends
But he said no,
And that's what life's all about bro!

Hamzah Ahmed (10)
Priory School, Slough

Best Friends For Life

Oh what joy it is
To have a friend like you
For giving me strength
The way you do.

For lifting me up
When I'm feeling down
And putting a smile on my face
When I'm wearing a frown.

Thanks for being there
And helping me grow
Your friendship means a lot
This I'd like you to know.

Many people will walk in and out of your life
But only true friends
Will leave footprints on your heart.

Sianna Amankwaah (10)
Priory School, Slough

Thank You Soldiers

We saw each admirable one of you,
At this special time
Because you served your nation
With so much pride,
In this unique way.

So, on this special day, we thank you
And we're as proud as can be,
Because you risked your life
For all of us and we are all free!

Thank you soldiers for serving your
Country for 100 years with so much confidence,
dedication and commitment.

Welcome back home soldiers.

Sohan Miseer (10)
Priory School, Slough

Devastating Dragons

D angerous, daring dragons soar through the night, cutting the wind with their fierce scales.
R oaring and raging across the pitch-black sky like male lions fighting to be alpha.
A tasty treat awaits them,
G orging on goats like you and I would with sweets,
O nward they go after this satisfying, scrumptious snack,
N apping first like babies, then they get up and go,
S wooping and swerving back home to their misty cove.

Olivia Prescott (8)
Priory School, Slough

Friendship

F riendship is fun, not,
R evolting,
I t's the time you spend with your friends,
E very second with your friend adds onto friendship,
N o time takes away your friendship,
D o nothing together, you'll make yourself lonely,
S tay together and you'll make more friends,
H appiness will follow you,
I n school, at home and wherever you go,
P eace will remain with you forever.

Khyla Powell Christian (8)
Priory School, Slough

The Moon And The Stars

In the dark of night
The moon is grey
The stars shine bright
But not in the day.

See the moon's glorious glow
Up and down below
Babies sleep with a star tune
Dawn will come very soon.

As we are asleep
And we fall so deep
The star and moon show
Display their wonderful glow.

In the dark of night
The moon's luminous white
Together it's extreme
Beauty will gleam.

Fariha Hamza (9)
Priory School, Slough

Weirdest Animals Around

There were very strange llamas,
Wearing pyjamas,
Jumping up and down.
Then we had the unicorns all being clowns,
Doing football fouls.
Then we had the foal
Who was singing a song
Which sounded like a howl.
Then we had the owl buzzing
Like a bee, oinking like a pig.
Then we had the dog who loved to dig, dig, dig
Which was very loud.
Finally we had the cow going moo, moo, moo,
Eating the grass going chew, chew, chew.

Tia Bradshaw (9)
Priory School, Slough

Don't Mine At Night!

If finding diamonds
In a cave system at night,
Beware of the mobs
As you might have to fight.
Gleaming ice blue in the dark,
You will seek.
Temptation and greed,
Won't set you free.
If mining at night,
Make sure you have armour.
For the greed of diamonds,
Makes for a poor farmer.
Beware of the mobs,
Secretly watching you mine.
Ready to attack in the moonlight,
Jealously guarding their shrine.

Phoebe Olivia Ward (9)
Priory School, Slough

Maths

Maths is my favourite lesson.
I hate English.
When I start maths I'm always excited
About what we are about to learn.
My favourite is chunking because it is very chunky
But English is not funky.
I try to do my best
But I lose less.
When I come into class
I just want to do maths.
Even when I struggle I play with rubble.
When I double I get in trouble.
It's time to run because I've done my work.

Josh Akerman (10)
Priory School, Slough

Seasons

If winter is a white blanket
And if autumn is a rainfall of colourful leaves
Not to forget,
If spring is an outburst of vibrant flowers,
So then, what is summer?

Summer is a warm season
Where all the flowers have bloomed
And leaves are back on trees.
Summer has clear skies and animals hunting.

But all seasons are beautiful,
Some more than others,
They bring joy and happiness to spread.

Mariam Hannah Khan (10)
Priory School, Slough

The Moon

The moon, an orb in the sky,
A mysterious sphere orbiting the Earth,
It is a beautiful dot of white paint,
A thumbprint on my ebony canvas.

It is a speck in the galaxy,
An ivory thief stealing the sun's light,
A beauty in the sky,
A natural guardian of the night.

A wonder like no other,
A defender, protecting us at sunset,
A glorious thing unlike another,
It is the wondrous moon.

Zara Khokhar (9)
Priory School, Slough

Georgie And Freddy The Dinosaur Brothers

Georgie roar, Georgie roar,
Georgie roar as loud as you can,
Georgie hunt, go hunt with Freddy.

Georgie eat a blanket of meat,
Georgie drag the meat to your cave,
Leave the rest for Freddy to eat,
Now go get hunting again.

Georgie eat your well-deserved meat,
Now leave the remains for me,
Go to your cave and get some sleep,
Now Georgie let me be free!

Sam Arbouch (11)
Priory School, Slough

My Dog

Black and white.
Thick and furry.
Fast as wind.
Always in a hurry.
Couple of spots.
Rubs my ear.
Always comes when he hears his name.
Loves his ball, it's his favourite thing.
What's fun for him?
Everything!
Great big tongue that licks my face.
Has a crate, his very own space.
Big brown eyes like moon pies.
He's my friend till the very end.

Daniyal Akram (9)
Priory School, Slough

Bully, Don't Be A Bully

Anyone can be bullied
Popular people, they just think they are in charge
Making up rumours that are not true
When the bully's job is done
With all that happening
You just want to hide in a dark corner,
Crying in a bath of your own tears.
Don't let bullies get to you,
And believe me you will get through it!
And you will make it to a happy future life.

Kylie Stanbridge (11)
Priory School, Slough

Happiness

Happiness isn't only a feeling,
It is a place!
So lift those rosy red cheeks
And put a smile on your face.
When I am happy and full of joy
You know, like when you get a fun toy!
School is great, my friends make me laugh,
Sadness is when my mum makes me have a bath.
So remember everyone,
Try not to be sad and glum,
Just smile and have amazing fun!

Daanya McCarroll (8)
Priory School, Slough

A Day At School!

Quick, quick, it's time to get up,
Brush my teeth, put on my clothes,
Have my breakfast and off I go.
5H is my class, my teacher is nice,
I spend the day learning, having so much fun.
Friday is my best day at school,
The lunch is yum.
I get a break,
But most of all I enjoy the time
Me and my friends meet.
Before I know it, it is time to go home.

Aadam Qamar (9)
Priory School, Slough

Flowers

A bunch of flowers,
Make my eyes so bright.

When they amazingly grow,
They're soft as snow,
They're multicoloured
Like a rainbow.

The lovely fragrance makes me sit and watch
For hours and hours,
These glamorous flowers are so nice,
They're so special.

You might think they're special
So do I!

Aleena Syed (8)
Priory School, Slough

My Caring Teacher

I drive to school with my mum
Looking forward to the day
With my caring teacher.
We line up with our teacher at the head of the line
With a big, gleaming smile.
Staring at each of us,
Looking forward to teaching us.
Sitting in class,
Shouting out our names for the register.
We all are looking forward to the rest of the day
With our caring teacher.

Kirandeep Kaur Dhillon (9)
Priory School, Slough

Girl Power

G irls have a strength
I know you may not see the length
R eally you should see
L ong as we may be

P owerful girls may be great
O therwise you will have no mates
W e all have a strength
E veryone sees how powerful we may be
R espect all the girls that use their time to be a flying bee!

Charlette Barton-Johnson (10)
Priory School, Slough

Butterfly

Swooping low,
Her wings like snow,
Diving to reach her goal,
Through the hole.

Clear of the hedge
And onto the edge
Of a tree
With birds and bees.

Looking out
There was no doubt
Of fun till dark
In a wildlife park.

Fun with friends,
It never ends,
Play till the night,
Make life bright.

Katie Emery (10)
Priory School, Slough

A Good Friend

There is nothing like a good friend
To tell your troubles to.
Someone to open up with,
Someone to talk you through,
The everyday struggle,
The help you get
And love you after all.

What joy it is,
To have a friend like you,
Lifting me up
When I'm feeling down,
Putting a smile on my face,
Your friendship means a lot.

Cynthia R Machokoto (9)
Priory School, Slough

The Crow

This creature has wings
And likes shiny things,
It flies in the air
Like a hot-air balloon, beware!

Its body is slim,
With a black shiny skin
And a long pointy beak
Just loved to fly to the peak.

Wandering here and there,
Chirping loud and clear,
What else could it be,
A crow! which fascinates me.

Muhammad Moiz Khan (7)
Priory School, Slough

Emotions That Hold You Together!

Happy,
Joyful and contented.

Sad,
Desolate and grieving.

Disgust,
Revolt and nausea.

Angry,
Enraged and irritated.

All the emotions hold you together
Either for your happiness, sadness,
Disgustedness or angriness.
Without these emotions you'll be...
Emotionless.

Khushi Mishra (10)
Priory School, Slough

All About Animals

Deep in the forest, looking for its prey,
With his glittering, piercing eyes,
He holds them in place.
Can you guess this mighty one?
It's Cheetah, the magnificent one.

Bouncing like a ball,
Hopping up and down,
Eating carrots,
All day long,
Can you guess it right?
Yes it's Mr Rabbit in flight!

Hira Basit (7)
Priory School, Slough

Hide Away

Creepers and spiders crawling in the night,
Wrapped in its own darkness,
Making me jump in a fright.

Pull out your weapons,
The diamond sword and pickaxe,
Light up your TNT and then fly away,
Only a few seconds before it all blows.
Build up your fort and hide away,
Wait till morning, when the sun starts to rise.

Haris Shakir (9)
Priory School, Slough

Gymnastics

I flipped so high on the bars
It felt like I had reached the stars!
I tumbled and flipped on the floor
And suddenly I felt I needed to do more.
Wobbling on the beam,
I felt I was in a dream.
Running towards the vault
I had suddenly come to a halt.
I had forgot to present.
I wondered, *would this be the end?*

Marley-Rose Larkins (9)
Priory School, Slough

The Unicorn Poem

The unicorns are in the sky.
The unicorns can fly ever so high.
The unicorns are in clouds.
The unicorns are coming down.

Unicorns have great big horns.
Unicorns' horns are as sharp as thorns.
Some people don't think unicorns are real
But I think they're the biggest deal!

Sharmaine Tianna Daryen Bevan (10)
Priory School, Slough

Anger

I am Anger,
I am red,
I have flaming fire,
I am as angry as Hell,
I am like a bomb dropping on a power station.

I am full of irritation,
My hair is getting messed up,
Like The Twits.

I am full of raging fire,
My mind is blowing like a tyre,
Why am I Anger?

Aminah Shakir (9)
Priory School, Slough

My Favourite Things

I like the colour pink,
It makes me think
Of all things I like to do.
The colour pink is shiny and bright
And makes me feel very great.
My favourite things are sweets,
They are my favourite treats,
They come in all different shapes,
Colours and sizes.
They are all my favourite treats.

Lexie Hiron (9)
Priory School, Slough

Emotions

You laugh when you're happy,
You cry a big flood of tears when you're sad,
You scream when you're scared.

All day,
All night,
Some day you'll give me a fright.

Your emotions change,
To a very strange moment,
I wonder what happens another day?

Lia Santucci (11)
Priory School, Slough

The Majestic Moon!

The moon

The moon is an illuminated, glistening disco ball, glistening at a fantastic party.
The moon is a delectable, fluffy marshmallow being devoured greedily by the mouth of a famished person.
As the moon rose to the sky, facing the Earth yet it can't say 'hi'.

Shamaila Khan (9)
Priory School, Slough

All About Me

I like to fly a kite
When the clouds are fluffy and white
Kites zooming
Colours booming.

I like drawing
Even if it's pouring.

When out in the sun
I like to run
Because it is fun.

I like to sing
Because it makes me relax.

Jessica Roberts (9)
Priory School, Slough

Autumn Days

As autumn arrived
the leaves from the trees
rustled and fell off.
The wind howled
as it rushed down the street.

We put on coats, gloves,
hats and boots.
We don't want to get a cold or flu
then we will be no good to run around
and have some fun!

Amina Irfan (10)
Priory School, Slough

Ice Cream

I ce-cold on your tongue
C reamy and delicious
E xciting flavours to choose from

C old sweetness in my mouth
R ushing down my throat
E asy to eat
A real sweet treat
M elts in my mouth like fire melts ice.

Rehaan Ali (10)
Priory School, Slough

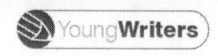

Dreams

Dreams are powerful
Dreams are you
Dreams are what you like to do
When you're sleeping, you are dreaming.

Dreams, dreams, dreams
Sometimes you dream
Sometimes you don't
Never give up on yours
And always hope
They will come true.

Caitlin Nsubuga (11)
Priory School, Slough

Animals

Animals are big, some animals are small,
Some are furry but not all.

Some are heavy, some are tall,
I bet you some animals can really fly.

Now you have heard the story of the animals,
This is how they are, this is how they live.

Naisha Mungur (10)
Priory School, Slough

Let's Celebrate 2017

The ball was blue
I sure knew what to do.
I kicked the ball high
Right up to the sky.
It came down to the ground
With a toe punt sound.
It went through the air,
Past their heads,
Hands held up.
We won the cup.
Let's cheer!

Amber-Lily Saunders (9)
Priory School, Slough

The Stars And The Wolf

The sky at night is dark
But tonight the stars shine bright.
Sometimes the clouds roll by
And shut the stars' light out.
But tonight the moon is high
And the wolf is running fast.
I can see his shadow moving,
Casting shadows on the moon.

Keelin Porter-Bull (10)
Priory School, Slough

Blocks

Blocks, blocks, what's the use?
Blocks, blocks, stack them up high or low
Or even in a row.
They're amazingly square
With no hair,
It's incredibly rare.
Remember to share!
Big or small,
Remember the rule...
Build!

Eryka Grace Richardson (8)
Priory School, Slough

Ghost

G hosts are far up in the sky with the power to fly
H elp them to escape this lie
O ptions that they can't deny, unusual sights seen by my eye
S trange things made by my mind
T en thousand ghosts, are they all kind?

Kiel Porter (10)
Priory School, Slough

Sweet Dreamz

I dream of chocolate cream,
Pink bees and sugar trees,
Bunnies bouncing,
Butterflies flying,
Gingerbread ground,
No sound,
Waterfall of coffee,
I've got toffee,
Don't fall asleep,
The dream is just beginning.

Alisha Rhea Khan (11)
Priory School, Slough

Rainbow Bright

When it rains and when it shines
A rainbow forms time to time.

Red and yellow and pink and green
All the wonderful colours you've seen.

In Irish legend it's been told
Find a leprechaun, find the gold!

Romany Donohoe-Flanders (7)
Priory School, Slough

My Life

I like to dance and sing
And take a lovely stroll in the park
I like to be creative
And draw lovely pieces of art
I like to be imaginative
Sometimes I am playful and silly
My favourite thing is everybody around me.

Saara Mahmood (9)
Priory School, Slough

Pinkie Pie

Although she likes to jump and play,
There's nothing that can stop her day,
Spinning round in circles so wide,
She likes to eat and likes to hide,
She likes to jump up and fly,
She's Pinkamena Dianna Pie.

Rudaina Khan (9)
Priory School, Slough

Amazing Computers

Computers are big,
Computers are small,
Computers are even on the wall,
Computers can be TVs, tablets and more.

Computers are cool,
Computers have keys,
Computers can be new
But never free.

Alex-David Wande (9)
Priory School, Slough

Halloween

Witches on broomsticks,
There's a chill in the air.
Skeletons and ghosts like to scare.
Pumpkins with candles
Give the sky a glowing night flare,
Children go trick or treating
With dark clothes.

Ben Carter (7)
Priory School, Slough

Running Around

I ran to a shop to get a mop
Then I ran to the park till it got dark.
I ran back home
Then I went to bed
Then I ran to my shed
Then my mum said to get her some food
Then I ran to the supermarket.

Mohamad Omar (8)
Priory School, Slough

Calico

There is a dog called Calico,
She is friendly, playful and funny,
Her nose is as wet as a fish,
Her eyes are as brown as a conker,
Her favourite game is chasing the ball,
She likes to play on grass.

Cameron Haines (10)
Priory School, Slough

Shayaan

Shayaan is cool,
Shayaan is small,
Shayaan likes to sing about school,
Shayaan likes swimming in a swimming pool.

I almost forgot,
He's the strongest amongst us all!

Shayaan Ahmed (9)
Priory School, Slough

Six Wives

Henry the Eighth, he had a great life
But I really wouldn't like to be his wife.
Catherine of Aragon was number one
But she lasted over 20 years before she was gone.
Next was Anne Boleyn
But sadly her head ended up in the bin.
After the death of Jane Seymour
Henry moved onto wife number four.
Anne of Cleves was wife number four
But before she could say anymore
She was divorced.
Next was Anne Boleyn's cousin,
Catherine Howard
But just another beheaded by the royal coward.
Henry's now died but Parr survived
And that's how the Stuarts arrived.

Lottie Stretton (8)
St Paul's Catholic Primary School, Tilehurst

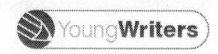

Why I Love Liverpool

Liverpool is my favourite football team
When I watch them, it's like a dream.
Sadio Mané is my favourite player for Liverpool,
Everyone likes him and he's really cool.
Anfield is where Liverpool play,
Jürgen Klopp, the manger, goes there every day.
We won the Championship League in 2005.
There was a great atmosphere, and it felt alive!
I am an amazing fan,
My whole family supports it,
Except for my nan!
Our manager, Jürgen Klopp,
Is the new king of the Kop!

Molly Clift (7)
St Paul's Catholic Primary School, Tilehurst

The Rapping Unicorns

In Lolly Land there's a unicorn,
Her name is Tilly.
With her twinkling, shimmering, glimmering horn
She was in a fight with Milly,
Because she thought she was the better one.
So they planned a rap battle.
Tilly's one was about the ice cream man
Milly's one was about some cattle.
So they picked the date for the fight,
Upon Shrewsbury Hill,
The time was set for the end of light,
The next morning it was time to fight.
The winner was Tilly the Mighty.

Sophia Armstrong (8)
St Paul's Catholic Primary School, Tilehurst

In My Bedroom

In my bedroom I will put the Eiffel Tower,
The Pyramids of Giza and the whole savannah.

In my bedroom I will put all the lights in the world,
The rainforests and Santa's sleigh.

In my bedroom I will put Lake Geneva,
An immaculate statue and the Taj Mahal.

In my bedroom I will put Wembley Stadium,
The O2 and Buckingham Palace.

In my bedroom, in my imagination,
The world is my oyster.

Harry Meaden (9)
St Paul's Catholic Primary School, Tilehurst

My Kitchen

In my kitchen I hear the popping of the toaster.
The pinging of the microwave.
The slamming of the fridge door.
The beeping of the oven.
This buzzing noise all around
Is quite an adventure all around
So listen out for the swishing
Of the washing machine
And dripping of the tap,
They all mix up as a jungle.
Kitchen sounds
And people talking in the background,
It's all quite magical.

Ava Slade (9)
St Paul's Catholic Primary School, Tilehurst

The Amazing Goalkeeper And His Sisters!

I'm big
I'm tall
But I'm only four foot small.
I stand between the sticks
And I do all my tricks.
I save all the goals
But sometimes they hit the poles.
When my team win
I have a great big grin.
It makes my Saturday great
But I am only eight.
My sisters like to dance,
My mum said it is by chance.
They start at two,
As soon as they can wear ballet shoes.

Charley Pearson (8)
St Paul's Catholic Primary School, Tilehurst

The Magical Unicorn

Unicorns are awesome
Unicorns are a magical sight
Unicorns are great
Unicorns are very bright.

Unicorns cross rainbows
Only when it's a sunny day
Come on everybody
It's time to play.

Unicorns are good
Unicorns are very fast
Unicorns are helpful
Unicorns are never last.

Alissa Shoefield (8)
St Paul's Catholic Primary School, Tilehurst

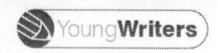

The Animal Jungle

When lions roar,
Eagles soar
And the dogs bark,
There is a snail that crawls
And a big whale shark.
So jaguars leap and kill a sheep,
Giraffes are as tall as a tree,
While horses are herbivores,
Pigs are omnivores,
The mice are very small
And not forgetting me!

Stephanie Adaugo Ugochukwu (7)
St Paul's Catholic Primary School, Tilehurst

At The Beach

At the beach I saw a boat set sail
A great big blue whale
And a mermaid flick its tail.

In the sand I played
With my brother's bucket and spade
Drinking ice-cold lemonade
And waving goodbye to the mermaid.

Erin Crawford (7)
St Paul's Catholic Primary School, Tilehurst

Popcorn

Sweet and salty,
Also yummy,
And so crunchy,
But the best place would be in my tummy.
All different flavours,
Popcorn is nutritious
And very tasty
But the best one is sweet and salty,
Very delicious!

Kayla Patton (8)
St Paul's Catholic Primary School, Tilehurst

The Ghost Busters

Ghostly night,
Pitch-black,
Scary Ghost Busters,
Come to fight back.
Rescue! Send them away!
Put on their protection packs
And save the day!

Callum Barrow (8)
St Paul's Catholic Primary School, Tilehurst

YoungWriters Est. 1991

YOUNG WRITERS INFORMATION

We hope you have enjoyed reading this book – and that you will continue to in the coming years.

If you're a young writer who enjoys reading and creative writing, or the parent of an enthusiastic poet or story writer, do visit our website **www.youngwriters.co.uk**. Here you will find free competitions, workshops and games, as well as recommended reads, a poetry glossary and our blog.

If you would like to order further copies of this book, or any of our other titles, then please give us a call or visit **www.youngwriters.co.uk**.

Young Writers
Remus House
Coltsfoot Drive
Peterborough
PE2 9BF
(01733) 890066
info@youngwriters.co.uk